John Day

Humour out of Breath

A Comedy Now first Reprinted from the Original Edition of 1608

John Day

Humour out of Breath
A Comedy Now first Reprinted from the Original Edition of 1608

ISBN/EAN: 9783744782074

Printed in Europe, USA, Canada, Australia, Japan

Cover: Foto ©Andreas Hilbeck / pixelio.de

More available books at **www.hansebooks.com**

HUMOUR OUT OF BREATH;

A COMEDY,

WRITTEN BY JOHN DAY;

NOW FIRST REPRINTED

FROM THE ORIGINAL EDITION OF 1608.

EDITED BY

J. O. HALLIWELL, ESQ., F.R.S.

LONDON:

PRINTED FOR THE PERCY LIBRARY.

1860.

Humour out of breath.

A Comedie

Diuers times latelie acted,

By the Children
Of
The Kings Reuells.

WRITTEN

BY

Iohn Day.

Printed at London for *Iohn Helmes,* and are to be sold
at his shop in Saint Dunstons Church-yard
in Fleet-street. 1608.

To Signior No-body.

WORTHLESSE *sir, I present you with these my vnperfect labours, knowing that what defect in me or neglect in the Printer hath left vnperfect, iudgement in you will winke at, if not thinke absolute. Being to turne a poore friendlesse childe into the world, yet sufficiently featur'd too, had it been all of one mans getting, (woe to the iniquitie of Time the whilest) my desire is to preferre him to your seruice: in which, as he shall be sure to get nothing, so likewise my hope is, he shall not loose much: For your bountie neither makes straungers loue you, nor your followers enuie you: you are a Patrone worthie the Sister-hood, I meane, the poore halfe dozen, for the Three Elders, they climbe aboue my element: the Sunne, the Moone, and the seuen Stars being scarce worthy the suruey of their workings: I protest I had rather bestow my paynes on your good worship for a brace of Angells certaine, then stand to the bountie of a Better-mans Purse-bearer, or a very good womans Gentleman-vsher: my reason is I cannot attend: your Bis dat, qui citò stands so like a Load-stone ouer your greate gate, that I feare twill drawe all the Iron-pated Muse-mongers about the towne in a short time to your patronage. For mine owne part I had rather bee yours volens, then be driuen nolens: So till I meete you next at your great Castle in Fish-street, ile neither taste of your bountie, nor be drunke to your health.*

One

of your first followers,

John Daye.

HUMOUR OUT OF BREATH.

ACTVS I.

SCENA I.

*Enter Octauio Duke of Venice, Hippolito and Francisco
his sonnes, Florimell his daughter: Hortensio
and others attendants.*

Octa. SONNES, hopefull buddes of fruitfull Italy,
Hauing banisht war, which like a prodigall
Kept wastfull reuells with our subiects bloud:
Since proude Anthonio our arch-enemy
Is in his iourney towards th'vnderworld,
Or houers in the shade of banishment;
Let vs in peace smile at our victory,
And euery brest passe his opinion
What pastime best becomes a conqueror.

  Fran. What sport but conquest for a conqueror?
Then with our wounds vndrest, our steeds still armd,
Branded with steele ere we wipe of the bloud
Of conquerd foes, lets with our shriller bugles
Summon the surly landlord of the forrest,

The kingly lyon, to a bloudy parle;
Combat the hart, the leopard or the bore,
In single and aduenturous hardyment:
The spirit of mirth in manly action rests,
Hauing queld men, lets now go conquer beasts.

   Oct. Manly resolu'd; Hippolitoes aduise.

   Hip. Rather like souldiers, and Octauioes sonnes,
Lets throw a generall challenge through the world,
For a proud turney, at the which our selues
Consorted with a hundred of our knights,
Accoutred like so many gods of warre,
Will keepe the lists gainst all aduenturers,
Which like the suns light figurd in a star
Should be a briefe epitome of war.

   Oct. Noble and royall, your opinion, daughter.

   Flo. Faith, I shall anger souldiers: I woulde poure
Spirit of life, *Aurum Potabile*,
Into the iawes of chap-falne schollership,
That haue since amorous Ouid was exild,
Lyen in a sowne. Y' aue many holds for war,
I would once view a garrison for witte:
Twere heauenly sport to see a traine of schollers
Like old traind soldiers skirmish in the schooles,
Trauerse their *Ergoes* and discharge their iests
Like peales of small-shot; were this motion granted
My selfe would be free woman of their hall,
And sit as sister at their festiuall.

Oct. Haue we not Padua ?

Flo. Yes, but the commaunders
Deale with our graduates, as the generall
Doth with his souldier, giues him place for fauoure,
Not for deseruing, looke intoo't your selfe,
You haue courts for tennis, and me thinkes t'were
Learning should not stand balling in the street [meet
For want of houseroome : oh tis much vnfit
Courtiers should be all pleasure and small wit.

Oct. All that you speake is but what we command.

Flo. But officers, father, cannot vnderstand
Their lords at first : wert not a gallant sight,
To see wits army royall come from fight ?
Some crownd with gold, others with wreath of bayes,
And whilst they hold their solemn holydaies,
Musick should like a louer court the skies,
And from the world wrest ringing plaudities.

Hip. My sister would make a rare beggar.

Fra. True, shee's parcell poet, parcell fidler already,
and they commonly sing three parts in one.

Oct. Wrong neither art nor musicke, they are twins
Borne and begot in heate, your thought of both.

Flo. I thinke, my lord, that musick is diuine,
Whose sacred straines haue power to combine
The soule and body ; and it reason beares,
For it is said that the celestiall spheres
Dance to Apolloes lyre, whose sprightly fires

Haue tamd rude beasts, and charmd mens wild
The author was immortall; the first strings [desires :
Made by a king, therefore an art for kings :
The world's a body, euery liberall art
A needfull member, musick the soule and hart.

   Oct. Well for hir sex hath Florimell discourst
Of heauenly musicke, and since all conclude
It is an art diuine, we were too rude
Should we reiect it ; musick, I take great pride
To heare soft musick and thy shrill voice chide. [skill,

   Flo. To please your grace, though I want voice and
Ile shew my selfe obedient to your will.   [*Sing.*

   Fra. This would haue done rare at a schollers
How do you like it, father?   [window,

   Oct. Highly, my boies, I rellish all delight,
For when the fiery spirit of hot youth
Kept house within me, I was all delight :
Then could I take my loue, no loue more fayre,
By the smooth hand, and gazing in loues ayre
Tell her her beauty beautifide the skie,
And that the sunne stole lustre from her eye.

   Fra. I do admire to heare my princely father
Thus merrilie discourse of trifling loue.

   Oct. Nay more, my boyes, when I was at your yeares,
I went a pilgrimage through Italie,
To find the shrine of some loue-hallowed saynt ;
Deuote to beauty, I would pray for loue;

Desiring beauty, I would sue for loue;
Admiring beauty, I would serue for loue :
Pray, sue, and serue, till beauty graunted loue.
If she denyd me, I would sweare she graunted ;
If she did sweare that she could neuer loue me,
Then would I sweare she could not chuse but loue me:
Let her sweare nere so much, still haue I sworne,
Till she had said I should not be forsworne.

Flo. I marry, brothers, here was cunning loue,
Learne like good schollers, heele make you wise in
He was a man in loue, were you such men ?   [loue :
Then were you men indeed, but boyes till then.

Fr. To please my father, ile inquest of beauty,
And neuer make returne till I haue found
A loue so faire, so rich, so honorable,
As fits the honor of Octauioes sonnes.

Hip. The like (you pleasd) vowes young Hippolito.

Oct. Doe, boyes, and I will teach you how to chuse them.
Elect not mongst whole troupes of courtly dames,
For amongst many, some must needs be ill :
The seld seene Phœnix euer sits alone,
Ioue courted Danae when she was alone :
Alone, my boyes, that is the only way,
Ladies yeeld that alone, they els say nay.

Flo. An expert souldier; how shall they choose them,

Oct. If her bright eye dim not the diamond; [father?
Say, it is bright, but brighter iems delight you,

If that her breath do not perfume the ayre;
Say, it is sweet, but sweeter sweets content you.
If that her cheeke compared to the lilly,
Make not the lilly black with whiter whitenesse;
Say it is lilly white, but black to white,
When your choise white must haue such high exceeds.

Flo. Father, you do exceed things possible;
Faith, say how many ladyes haue you seene,
Much fayrer then my selfe, in all your trauayle ?

Oct. Should the crow teach me, then no lady fayrer;
If iudgement tell me, then a many fayrer :
Thou art myne owne, I must thinke well of thee,
Yet, Florimella, many doe excell thee.

Flo. Should the crow teache, I am not all crow
Though iudgement, I not all perfection black; [black.
Though you haue seen ladyes that dim the day,
Yet will I think my selfe as fayre as they.

Oct. Doe, Florimella, and ile one day get
A husband for thee, that shall thinke thee fayre.

Flo. And tyme ifaith, that prety sport would be,
Wiue it for them, you shall not husband me.

Oct. Yet you will take my counsell in your choise.

Flo. Yes, if I had not yeares ynough to choose,
Would you direct me as you doe your sonnes ?
With, Daughter, take a man with such a nose,
With such an eye, with such a colour beard,
Thus big, thus tall, with all his teeth afore ;

Thus lipt, thus legd, thus handsome, thus apparrelld.

Were not this pittiful ? o pittifull :

Now by the soule of soule-commaunding loue,

I will not stoope to such obedience,

I must be bid to blush when I am kist,

Bid my loue welcome, and I thank you, sir ;

With no, indeed, I know not what loue is,

I neuer heard so much of loue before,

I pray take heede, nay, fie you goe too far ;

With such a rabble of prescriptions,

As neuer mayd of a conceiuing spirit

Will follow them ; yet, brothers, goe you on,

Take you good counsell, Florimell will none.   [*Exit.*

   Oct. I, daughter, are you so experiencd ?

An elder woman might haue spoken lesse.

Yet by your leaue, mynion, ile watch you so,

Your I shall still be gouernd by my no.

But come, my sonnes, take patterne of great Ioue,

Early ith' morning suit your selues for loue. [*Exeunt.*

Enter Anthonio Duke of Mantua, Hermia and Lucida
   his daughters ; they with angels, and he with a net.

   Ant. Go, daughters, with your angels to the brooke,

And see if any siluer-coated fish

Will nibble at your worme-emboweld hooks :

Deceiue the watry subiects, yet the name

Of foule deceit, me thinks, should fray them from you.

Alack, alack, I cannot blame the world,
That in the world there is so much deccipt;
When this poore simple trade must vse deccipt.
But with what conscience can I make this net,
Within whose meshes all are caught that come:
They cousen one at once, this cousens many,
I will vndoo't, it shall not cousen any.
But, daughters, go practise that little sinne,
Ile mend this great fault ere the fault begin.
O, cousening fortune, how hast thou decciu'd me!
Turning me out a doores to banishment,
And made another lord of Mantua.
I that was lord now slaue to misery.

Her. Take comfort yet, deare father.

Ant. Comfort? no:
My brest's turnd prison, my proude iaylor, woe,
Locks out all comfort: whers your valiant brother?

Her. All discontent, like to a wounded lyon
He forrages the woods, daring proude fortune
At her best weapon; he accounts this smart
As a slight hurt, but far off from the hart.

Anth. How holds his humour?

Inc. The same fashion still:
But somwhat sadder-colourd, death may end
But neuer change him, see our words haue raisd him.

[*Enter Aspero.*

Anth. Fitly applide, for a walks like a ghost.

Why, how now, sonne?

Asp. Peace.

Her. Brother.

Asp. Good now, peace,
Wake me not, as you loue me.

Luc. What a sleepe?

Asp. I, in a most sweet sleepe, blisters o' your tongues for waking me.

Anth. Thou forgettest thy selfe.

Asp. I should not be a courtier els; mee thought I was at a strange wedding.

Anth. Prithee, what wedding?

Asp. Of a young lawyer and old Madam Conscience.

Anth. I scarce beleeue that.

Asp. Nor I neither, because it was a dreame; but mee thought the yong man doted on the old woman exceedingly.

Anth. That was miraculous! Did they liue together?

Asp. In the country they did, and agreed passing well all the long vacation; and but for two things, he would haue carried her vp to the terme with him.

Ant. What things were those?

Asp. One was, because her gowne was of the old fashion; the other was, cause he would not haue her by when he took fees.

Ant. His reason for that?

Asp. For feare if a bribe had bin offered, she being by, he shold haue had the bad conscience to take it.

Anth. His wife and he liued together.

Asp. Conscience and the lawyer, as louingly as men and their wiues do, one flesh, but neither medle nor make one with another.

Ant. Man and wife part, thats strange!

Asp. O lord, sir, profit can part the soule and the body, and why not man and wife; now you haue had my dreame, father, let me vnderstand yours.

Anth. How can he dreame that neuer sleeps, my sonne?

Asp. O, best of all: why, your old world doth nothing but dreame: your machiauell he dreames of state, deposing kings, grounding new monarchies: the louer hee dreames of kisses, amorous embraces: the newe-married wife dreames, that rid of her young husband she hugs her old loue, and likes her dreame well ynough too: the country gentlewoman dreams that when her first husband's dead, she marries a knight, and the name of Lady sticks so in her mind that shees neuer at hearts-case till she get her husband dub'd; the captaine, he dreames of oppressing the souldiers, deuising stratagēs to keep his dreame, and that dreame wakes in the pate of Octauio your arch-enemy, who is not content to hurle vs into the

whirlepoole of banishment, but binds waights at our
heeles, leaden pouerty, to sinke vs to the very depth
that we should neuer rise againe.

Her. Then since all dreame, let vs dreame of
reuenge.

Asp. I, marry, sister, that were a dreame worth
dreaming, and ile sleepe out my braines but ile compasse it.

Anth. Pretty content; we kill our foes in dreames.

Asp. Vds foot, ile doe it waking then.

Anth. Aspero.

Asp. At counsell table.

Anth. Heare me.

Asp. In his dutches armes, twere base to go disguisd,
No, my reuenge shall weare an open brow;
I will not play the coward, kill him first
And send my challenge after; ile make knowne
ˌMy name, and cause of comming, if I thought
Griefe like a painter had so spoyl'd my visage
He could not know me, on my breast ide write
How ere I am disfigured through woe,
I am the thing was made for Aspero.
Speake not, I am as constant as the center;
Some fortune, good or bad, doth beckon me,
And I will run, bitter reuenge tasts sweete :
If nere on earth farewell, in heauen weele meete.
Attendance, sirra, your low commedie

Craues but few actors, weele breake company.

Anth. As many blessings as the sea hath sands [*Exit*
Attend thee in thine honorable iourney :   *cum Puero*
Come, pretty maides, we haue not wrought to day,
Or fish, or fast, our neede must needs obey. [*Exeunt.*

Enter Hippolito, Francisco, Florimell, and Page
meeting them.

Fr. Now, sirra, what haue you been about ?

Page. About my liuing, sir.

Hip. Whats that ? feeding ?

Pa. No, sir, looking into the vnderofficers about the
court.

Hip. Canst get any liuing out of them ?

Pa. I, sir, my betters get good liuings out of officers, and why not I ? but to be plaine, I haue bin
seeking your good lordship.

Fr. But your boyship hath so sought vs, that wee
haue found you.

Page. Will you sell your findings, my lord ?

Hip. They are scarce worth giuing.

Flo. Yes, a boxe to keepe them in, for feare you
loose them againe.

Pa. And I were a man as I am no woman, id'e
pepper your box for that icast.

Flo. You icast.

Pa. In earnest law I would, madam.

Fr. Well, sir, no more, here comes our royall father.

Enter Octavio, Hortensio, Flamineo, etc.

Oct. How now, my boyes? prouided for your
   iourney?

Beauty conduct you: what, attyrd like shepheards?

I thought t'haue seene you mounted on your steeds,

Whose fiery stomackes from their nostrills breath

The smoke of courage, and whose wanton mouthes

Do proudely play vpon their yron bits:

And you in stead of these poore weeds in robes,

Richer then that which Ariadne wroughte,

Or Cytharaes aery-mouing vestment.

Thus should you seeme like louers suited thus,

Y'oude draw faire ladies harts into their eies,

And strike the world dead with astonishment.

   Fr. Father, such cost doth passe your sons reuenues.

We take example from immortall Ioue,

Who, like a shepheard, would repaire to loue.

   Oct. And, gentle loue conduct you both, my sonnes;

Daughter, go bring them onward in their way.

Were not we cald back by important busines,

We would not leaue you thus: Hortensio,

Is my disguise prepard, for I vnknowne

Will see how they behaue themselues in loue.

   Hort. Tis done, my lord.

   Oct. Once more, my boyes, adieu:

He sends you forth that meanes to follow you.

                                        [*Exit.*

Flo. Now, brothers, you must amongst these wenches,
Faith, for a wager which shall get the fairest?

Fr. Ile gage a 100. crownes mine proues the fairest.

Hip. A match, ile venter twice so much of mine.

Flo. And ile lay gainst you both, that both your
loues, get them when you can, where you can, or how
you can, shall not be able to compare with me in
beauty.

Fran. That wager ile take, for tis surely won.

Hip. Las, thou art but a star to beauties sun.

Flo. Star me no stars, go you and stare for loue,
Ile stay at home, and with my homely beauty
Purchase a loue, shall thinke my looks as faire,
As those faire loues that you shall fetch so far;
But take your course, fate send you both faire lucke.

Fr. How if't be fowle?

Flo. Nay, ift be forked, you must beare it off with
head and shoulders.

Fr. Oh stale, that icast runs oth' lees.

Flo. You must consider tis drawne out of the bottome of my witte.

Fr. O shallow wit, at the bottome so soone.

Flo. Deepe ynough to lay you in the mire.

Page. Or els tis shallow indeede, for they are
foundred already, but I must play dun, and draw
them all out o'th mire.
Whats a clock, my lord?

Flo. Which of them dost aske ? thou seest they are two.

Pag. What two are they, madam ?

Flo. Why two fooles.

Fr. Is it not past two? doth it not come somewhat neere three, sister ?

Page. Shew perryall and tak't; but come, my lord, you haue stood fooling long ynough, will you about your busines in good earnest ?

Fra. Indeed we will.

Flo. And they are deeds you must trust too, for women will respect your words but slitely without deeds.

Page. Why are women called angells, but because they delight in good deeds, and loue heauen, but that it will not be won without them ?

Fr. They shall haue deeds.

Flo. Brother, and good deeds too :
They are tongues that men must speake with when
                they wo.

Hip. That tongue weel practise; sister, to loue we
        leaue you.   [*Exeunt brothers.*

Flo. Louers, take heede least cunning loue deceiue
        you.   [*Exit with Page.*

            Finis actus primi.

ACTVS SECVNDVS.

Enter Octauio disguised, Hortensio, Flamineo.

Oct. No more ; thus suted ile attend my sonnes.
Impute it not to any ruffian vaine,
But to a fathers wakefull prouidence.
Louers like bees are priuiledgd to tast
All buds of beauty ; should they chance to light
Vpon some worthles weed ile hinder it :
The cies of youth will now and then dwell there
Whereas they should not glance ; this doubt I feare.

Fla. And well aduisd, my liege ; should they incline
To loue not fitting their estates and births,
You with your present counsell may preuent them.

Oct. Thats my intent ; and further, in my absence
I leaue my land and daughter to thy charge.
The girle is wanton ; if she gad abroad
Restraine her, bound her in hir chamber dore ;
My word's thy warrant, let her know so much :
Farewell, at home I leaue my feare with thee,
And follow doubt abroad.

Hor. Ile carefull be.   [*Exeunt.*

Oct. Now to my busines ; I haue a strange habit,
and I must cut out an humour sutable to it, and
humours are pickt so neere the bone, a man can scarce
get humour ynough to giue a flea his breakfast : but I

am a stale ruffian, my habit is braue, and so shall my
humor be, and here comes one to giue me earnest of it.

Enter Aspero and his boy.

Asp. Send him a letter that I come to kill him.

Boy. Twere great valor, but little polticy, my lord.

Asp. How long haue you bin a matchiauilian, boy?

Boy. Euer since I practisd to play the knaue, my
lord.

Asp. Then policy and knauery are somewhat a kin.

Boy. As neere as penury and gentry, a degree and
half remou'de, no more.

Asp. How came in the kindred twixt gentry and
penury?

Oct. Shall I tell you, sir?

Asp. First, tell me what thou art?

Oct. Lyme and haire; playster of Paris, kneaded
together with rye dowe and goats milke; I am of a hot
constitution, wonnot freeze.

Asp. Thy profession.

Oct. A foole or a knaue, choose you which.

Boy. Then thou art fit for any gentlemans company.

Oct. True, boye, for your sweete foole and your fine
knaue are like a paire of vpright shooes, that gentlemen weare so long, now of one foote, then of another,
till they leaue them neuer a good soale.

Asp. That makes your foole and your knaue haue such bad soales; but what dost thou seeke?

Oct. Mine owne vndoing, sir,—seruice.

Asp. Indeed seruice is like the common law, it vndoes any one that followes it long. Canst describe seruice?

Oct. Yes, tis a vacant place, fild vp with a compleate knaue, a miserable pandar, or an absolute beggar.

Asp. Your opinion, boy?

Boy. I say a seruingman is an antecedent.

Oct. Because he sits before a cloakebag.

Boy. He is likewise a nominatiue case, and goes before his mistrisse.

Oct. Thats when the verbe he goes before, his mistrisse, and he can agree togither.

Boy. If not, he turnes accusatiue and followes his master.

Asp. Woot follow me, fellow?

Oct. To a tauerne, and thou woot pay for my ordenary.

Asp. My businesse is more serious, thou dost not know me.

Oct. Nor my selfe neither, so long as I haue maintenance.

Asp. Didst neuer heare of the wars betwixt Venice and Mantua?

Oct. I cut some few of the Mantuans throates.

Asp. And wert not a knaue for't?

Oct. No, I was a Venetian commander, a great man. The reason of this question?

Asp. Dost know the Duke of Venice?

Oct. I am his right hand.

Asp. Woot do me a message to him?

Oct. What is't?

Asp. Tell him I hate him; my name's Aspero; has banisht my father, vsurps his dukedome, and I come to be reuengd.

Oct. Anthonioes sonne? vesfoot, hast any gold?

Asp. Thy reason?

Oct. Shalt be reuengd. Giue me money, ile be thy snaile and score out a siluer path to his confusion.

Asp. No, my reuenge shall be like my fathers wrongs, *in aperto:* lend me any honest aide.

Oct. Pax of honesty, it goes a begging vpon crutches; and can get reliefe out of few but schollers. I shall not kill him?

Asp. Ide be thy death first.

Oct. Yet, you say you hate him.

Asp. Equall with my shame.

Oct. Make him chew a bullet then.

Asp. No, though my state with pouerty be tainted,
Mine acts and honor shall liue still acquainted.

Oct. True moulded honor: I admire the temper
Of thy mild patience; that not all the wrongs

I layd vpon thee can enforce thy spleene
To fowle requitall: had thy comming tane
Any base leuell, it had cost thy life ;
But beeing free, and full of honour, liue ;
Thy vertues teach me honor; freely goe,
A secret friends worse then an open foe.
You are too honest for my attendance; farewell, sir.

Asp. And thou too knauish for my employment.
But here comes more company.

Enter Florimell and Page.

Flo. Boy, let your attendance waite further of,
Vnder this shade I meane to take a sleepe.

Pa. And may you, madam, like a souldier sleepe.

Flo. How, boy, in alarums ?

Pag. No, ladye, but in armes, and you had neede of
them too; for see the enemy comes downe. Shall I
sound a parlee ?

Flo. Peace, wag.

Pa. Peace! O coward, offer peace and but two to
two of them.

Flo. Boy, dost know what gentleman it is ?

Pa. Gentle madam, no; but he is a man.

Flo. Beleeue me, boy, he is a proper man.

Pa. Man is a proper name to a man, and so he
may be a proper man.

Flo. I loue him, hees a very proper man.

Pa. She loues him for his properties, and indeede many women loue men only to make properties of them.

Flo. Pray, gentleman, if no more, tell me where you were born.

Asp. Faire virgine, if so much, no where, some where, any where, where you would haue me.

Flo. Faith, I would haue it.

Asp. Marry, and you shall haue it, ladie.

Flo. What shall I haue, sir?

Asp. Why, a kisse.

Flo. Nothing els: we courtiers count them trifles, not woorth taking.

Asp. Why then, bestow one of mee; ile take it most thankfully.

Flo. I wil not stand with you for a trifle, sir; pray where were you borne?

Asp. In Italy, but neuer yet in Venice.

Flo. You may in Venice; gentle sir, adieu. [*Exit.*

Asp. Gentle lady, thrice as much to you.

Pa. Farewell, sweet heart. [*Exit.*

Boy. God a mercy, bagpudding.

Asp. You may in Venice; gentle sir, adieu. This begets wonder.

Boy. Yare not wise then; what do you take her for?

Asp. Some great woman.

Boy. Some woman great with child. Be ruld; shees a pynk. Board her.

Asp. But how? the meanes.

Boy. Make but a shotte of flattery at hir broad side, and sheele strike saile presently.

Asp. Flattery?

Boy. I, flattery; women are like fidlers; speake them faire theile play of any instrument.

Asp. I, that they can play of.

Boy. Shees a botcher cannot play a little of all.

Asp. And to common that wil play too much of any; but come, ile vse meanes to get her.

Boy. Nay, you must first haue meanes to giue her.

Asp. Why, in the course of schollership the genitiue case goes before the datiue.

Boy. The grammarians are fooles that plac'de them so; for *in Rerum Natura* the datiue goes before the genetiue; you must alwayes giue before you can get; louers are fooles, and fooles must be liberall.

Asp. Will not women respect a man for his good parts?

Boy. Yes, some few; but all for his good guiftes. A gentleman with his good guifts sit at the vpper end of the table on a chayre and a cushion, when a scholler with his good partes will be gladde of a ioynd stoole in the lobby with the chambermaids.

Asp. I will haue good guifts and shew my selfe liberall to, though I beg for't.

Boy. I thinke that will be the end; for penury has
tane a lease of your pocket to keep court in this
Christmasse.

Asp. Well, how so ere, shee's faire and courteous,
And courteous faire is a faire guift in ladies:
She may bee well discended; if shee be,
Shee's fit for loue, and why not then for me. [*Exeunt.*

Boy. And you be not fitted in Venice tis straunge,
for tis counted the best flesh-shambles in Italie: but
heer's no notable coward, that hauing suffered wrong
by a man, seeks to right himselfe of a woman. [*Exit.*

Enter Hippolito Francisco, like shepheards,
Octauio in disguise.

Oct. Looke you, sir, I am like an Irish beggar, and
an English bur, will sticke close where I finde a good
nap; I must and will dwell with you.

Fr. What canst do?

Oct. Still *Aquauitæ*, stampe crabs, and make mus-
tard; I can do as much as all the men you keepe.

Fra. Prithee, what?

Oct. Why vndo you, and twenty could do no more.
But busines; come, my wits grow rusty for imployment.

Fr. Canst keepe counsell?

Oct. My mother was a midwife.

Hip. Hast any skill in loue?

Oct. I am one of Cupids agents; haue *Ouids Ars*

Amandi ad vngues; know *causam,* and can apply *remedium,* and minister *effectum* to a haire. But why do you aske? haue you trauerst an action in loues spirituall court?

Fra. Not to dissemble, we haue.

Oct. And without dissembling, youle neuer come out of it; but tell me true, are you in loue already? or haue you but desire to bee in loue?

Fra. Indeed I am in loue to be in loue.

Hip. And I desire to liue in fond desire,
And yet I doubt to touch blind fancies fier.

Oct. Tis good to doubt, but tis not good to feare,
Yet still to doubt will at the last proue feare;
Doubt loue, tis good, but tis not good to feare it,
Loue hurts them most, that least of all come neere it.

Fr. Then to doubt loue is the next way to loue.

Oct. Doubtles it is, if you misdoubt not loue.

Hip. Doubt and misdoubt, what difference is there
    here?

Oct. Yes, much : when men misdoubt, tis sayd they
    feare.

Fra. But is it good in loue to be in doubt?

Oct. No, not in loue, doubt then is iealousie :
Tis good to doubt before you be in loue;
Doubt counsells how to shun loues misery.

Fra. Your doubtfull counsell counsells vs to loue.

Oct. To equall loue, I like experience speake.

Hip. Experiencd louer, you haue spoken well.

Oct. Experience wanting louers, truth I tell,
Yong wits be wise, in loue liue constant still,
You need nor doubt good hap, nor misdoubt ill.

Enter Lucida and Hermenia with angles

And see, your discourse has coniured vp beauty in the
likenesse of two countrimaides, but you shall not come
in the circles of their armes, if I can keepe you out.

Fra. These are too meane for loue; brother, lets
leaue them.

Oct. What, speechles? will you make dumbe virgins
of them?

Hip. Oh, we are sonnes of a great father.

Oct. So is the sun of heauen, yet hee smiles on the
bramble as well as the lilly; kisses the cheeke of
a beggar as louingly as a gentlewoman, and tis good
to imitate him, tis good.

Her. Say, sister, had we not fine sport to day?

Luc. We had, if death may be accounted play.

Her. Why, tis accounted pleasure to kill fish.

Luc. A pleasure nothing pleasant to the fish.

Her. Yet fishes were created to be kild.

Luc. Cruell creation then, to haue liues spild.

Her. Their bodies being food, maintaine our breath.

Luc. What bodies then haue we, to liue by death?

Her. Come, come, you vainely argue; it is good.

Luc. What, is it good to kill? oh God, oh God.

Her. If it be sin, then you your self's a sinner.

Luc. I thank proud fortune for't, my woes beginner.

Oct. Foot, are yee not ashamd to stand by like idle ciphers, and such places of account voyde? and they had bin rich offices, and you poore courtiers, you would haue bin in them in halfe the time.

Fra. Though against stomack.—

Oct. Nothing against stomack, and you loue me.

Hip. Faire maids, if so you be, you are well met.

Her. Shepheards, or be what els you are, well met.

Fra. Tis well, if that well met we be to you.

Luc. If not to vs, you are vnto your selues.

Hip. We did not meet, you saw vs come togither.

Her. What ere we saw, you met ere you came
            hither.

Fr. We did, we met in kindred, we are brothers.

Luc. So, shepheards, we did meet, for we are sisters.

Hip. Then, sisters, let vs brothers husbands be.

Her. So, brothers, without our leaues you well may

Fr. Say, we desire to husband it with you.   [be.

Luc. Know we desire no husbands such as you.

Hip. A shepheard is an honest trade of life.

Her. Yet honest shepheard has with honest trade
            some strife.

Hip. He seldome sweares but by his honesty.

Her. So honest men do too aswell as he.

Fr. But will you trust a shepheard when he vowes?

Luc. No, neuer ; if his oath be that he loues.

Hip. Yet if I sweare, that needs must be mine oath.

Her. Sweare not, for we are misbeleeuers both.

Fr. Let vs perswade you to beleeue we loue you.

Luc. First, we intreat you giue vs time to proue you.

Hip. Take time, meane time weele praise yee to our powers.

Her. Oh time, sometime shepheards haue idle howers.

Fra. Ile say thy cheek no naturall beauty lacks.

Luc. Good, if it had bin spoke behind our backs.

Hip. Ile say this is the heauen of heauenly graces.

Her. O heauen, how they can flatters to our faces.

[*Exeunt.*

Fr. Brother, the last is fayrest in my eie.

Hip. I, but the first, brother, is first in beauty.

Fr. First in your choice, but not in beauty, sir.

Oct. Come yee so neere as choice : then tis time for mee to stop, for feare the musick run too far out of tune. How now, gallants, in dumps ?

Fr. No, but in loue.

Oct. Thats a dumpe, loues nothing but an Italian dumpe or a French brawle.

Hip. Me thinkes tis sweeter musicke.

Oct. And twere in tune, I confesse it; but you take your parts too low, you are trebble courtiers, and will neuer agree with these country mynnikins; the musickes too base, neuer meddle in't.

Fra. Peace, doatard, peace ; thy fight of loue is

Thou canst not see the glory of loues sunne :　　[done,

Spent age with frosty clowds thy sight doth dim,

That thou art blind to see, and apt to sin.

　　Oct. Is it accounted sin to speak the truth ?

　　Hip. And worse, when age spits poyson against youth.

　　Oct. They do not fit your callings; let them go.

　　Fr. Yet they are faire. We loue; thou art loues foe.

　　Oct. I am your friend, and wish you from this loue.

　　Hip. Canst thou heaue hills? then thou my thoughts maist moue.

But neuer els.

　　Oct.　　Neuer ?

　　　　　　　Fr. No, neuer.

　　　　　　　　　　Oct. Stay.

Hip. We are bound for loue.

　　　　　　　Oct. Hate.

　　　　　　　　　　Fra. Hinder not our way.

　　　　　　　　　　　　[Exeunt brothers.

　　Oct. I, boyes; will eagles eglets turne to bastards?

Then must I change my vaine, and once more proue,

To teach you how to hate aswell as loue.　　*[Exit.*

　　　　　　Finis Actus Secundi.

ACTVS TERTIVS.

Enter Page and Florimell.

Pa. SWEET hony candy madam, if it be no forfeit to tell tales out of Cupids free schoole, tell what proficient your louer Aspero proues?

Flo. Now, so loue helpe me loe, a passing weake one and verye vnready.

Pag. The better, for women would haue their louers vnreadye to choose.

Flo. How ready you are to play the knaue! But to Aspero.

Pa. I do not thinke but thers good musick in him; your tongue harps so much vpon his name.

Flo. I shall neuer forget him.

Pa. I faith, lady, then I know what I know.

Flo. What do you know, I pray?

Pa. Marry, that if you neuer forget him, you shall euer remember him. Was he neuer in your chamber?

Flo. Yes, but he shewed himselfe the strangest foole. And by my troth, loe, I am sorry for't too. I had as good an appetite to maintaine discourse.—But here a comes. If euer I choose a man by the fulnesse of his calfe, or a cock by the crowing—Looke, and the bash-full foole do not blush already.

Pa. You may do well to kisse him, and make him bold, madam.

Pa. Boy, go know what strange gentleman that is?

Asp. Slid, what a strange lady's this? Madam, though I seeme a stranger to you, I lay with one last night that's well acquainted with you.

Flo. Acquainted with me?

Asp. And knowes you, and loues you, and you loue him, and haue bestowed kind fauours of him to.

Flo. I bestow fauors! What fauours?

Asp. Though twere but a trifle, he tooke it as kindly as some would haue done a kisse.

Flo. Lord, what a while this iest has bin a brooding! and it proues but addle, too, now it is hatched.

Asp. Tis a pig of your owne sow, madam; and I hope your wit will bestow the nursing of it.

Flo. So it had need, I thinke; tis like to haue but a drie nurse of yours.

Pa. O, drie ieast! all the wit in your head will scarce make sippits in't. What, a ground, and such a faire landing place? get a shore, or be rankt amongst fooles for euer.

Flo. And faith, ist not pitty such a proper man should keepe company with a foole.

Asp. I keepe company with none but you, lady.

Flo. You keepe mine against my will.

Asp. So do I the fooles, I protest; but take away yours, ile soone shift away the fooles.

Pug. I haue not scene a foole so handsomely shifted in Venice.

Asp. But come, shall the foole and you bee friends?

Flo. The foole and I? y' are too familiar.

Asp. Why, I hope a foole may be a ladies familiar at all times.

Flo. Come, y' are too saucy.

Asp. Indeed, tis a fooles part of Ione to be in the sauce afore my lady; otherwise, I am neither foole nor saucy.

Flo. Not, proude sir?

Asp. Not, coy lady; come, why should your tongue make so many false fiers that neuer come from your heart? you loue me, I know you louo me; your spirit, your looke, your countenance bewrayes it.

Flo. You icast.

Asp. In earnest you do, and you shall know't in earnest too; lend me this iewell.

Flo. Iewell? away, you sharking companion.

Asp. How?

Flo. Wandring strauagant, that like a droane flies humming from one land to another.

Pa. Slight, and thou hast any wit, now shew her thy sting.

Flo. And lightst vpon euery dayry maid and kitchen-wench.

Asp. And now and then on a ladies lip, as——

Flo. You did of mine, you would say; and I am hart sory you can say it; and when by your buzzing flattery you haue suckt the smallest fauour from them, you presently make wing for another.

Asp. Marry, buz.

Flo. Double the zard, and take the whole meaning˙ for your labour.

Pa. The buzzards wit's not so bald yet, I tro.

Asp. A word in your care, madam; the buzzard will anger you.

Flo. With staying, you do.

Asp. With going, I shall.

Flo. Away.

Asp. I away; neuer intreat, tis too late : if you send after me, I wil not come back; if you write to me, I will not answer; drowne your eyes in teares, I will not wipe them; breake your heart with sighes, I will not pitty you: neuer looke, signes cannot moue me; if you speake, tis too late; if you intreate, tis bootles; if you hang vpon me, tis needlesse; I offred loue, and you scornd it; my absence will be your death, and I am proud ont'.   [*Exit.*

Flo. Is he gon, boy?

Pa. Yes faith, madam.

Flo. Cleane out of sight?

Pag. And out of mind to, or els you haue not the mind of a true woman.

Flo. Thou readst a false comment, boy; call him againe; yet doe not, my heart shall breake ere it bend.

Pa. Or els it holdes not the true temper of woman-
hood; but faith, tell me, madam, do you loue him?

Flo. As a Welchman doth toasted cheese; I cannot dine without him; hee's my pillow, I cannot
sleep quietly without him; my rest, I cannot liue
without him.

Pa. O that he knew it, lady.

Flo. He does; he would neuer haue left me els.
He does.

Pa. You calld him foole, but me thinks he prooues
a physitian, has found the disease of your liuer by the
complexion of your lookes; but see, he returnes.

Enter Aspero meditating.

Flo. And now, me thinks, I loath him more then I
lou'd him; goe run for Hortensio my guardian, bid
him come armd; ther's intent of treason, tell him.

Pa. My lady cannot choose but dance well, shees
so full of prety changes. [*Exit.*

Flo. I wonder you dare come in my sight, consider-
ing the wrong you did me.

Asp. I came I confesse, but with no intent to see
you I protest, and that shall be manifested by the
shortnes of my stay.

Flo. Tis too long and twere shorter then tis, will he
not court me? not? nor speak to me neither? nay
neuer ask pardon, tis to late, we shall ha' you come to

my window one of these mornings with musicke ; but
doe not, my patience is to much out of tune ; out of
my sight I hate thee worse then I loath painting ; I
hate thee, out of my sight.

Asp. Inough, will you be a quiet woman yet ? will
you, speake afore my resolue take strength ? will
you, do but say you are sorry, I aske no mends but
a kisse, kindly, come : shall I hat'e ?

Flo. Ile kisse a toad first.

Asp. You will ; remember this another time, a toade
you will : I know thou lou'st me, and I see the pride
of thy humour ; I doe, and thou shalt know I doe ;
halfe an hower hence wee shall haue you weeping on
your knees, with O my Aspero, would I had died
when I reiected thee, but doe, weepe till I pitty thee ;
a tooad! Ile make thee creepe on thy knees for
a kisse.

Flo. You will.

Asp. Thy bare knees, I will, and goe without it to.

Flo. Out humourd ? O, I would sell my part of
immortality.

Asp. But to touch my hand, thou wouldst, I know
thou woldst.

Flo. O how spleene swells mee ! Helpe, Hortensio ; creepe a my knees ? Hortensio.

Enter Hortensio with his man Assistance.

Hort. How fares my beautious charge ? weeping.

lady? The law shall fetch red water from his veynes that hath drawne bloud of your eies; is this the traytor?

Asp. Traytor! in thy disloyall throte thou liest.

Pa. O monstrous, a wishes you choakt, my lord.

Hort. How? choakt?

Pa. I, choakt; for a wishes the traytor in your throate; and hee's a very small traytor that is not able to choake a wiser man then your lordship.

Hort. Downe with him.

Pa. I, downe with him, if he stick in your throat, and spare not.

Flo. Do not kill him; though hee deserues death, yet doe not kill him, onely disweapon him; so.

Hor. But, madam.

Flo. I will not heare him; keepe him; but keepe him safe on your liues; if he get away or miscarry in prison, as I am heire of Venice, Ile haue your heads for't.   [*They bind him.*

Hort. I warne you, madam, if yrons will hold him.

Flo. Fie, fie, with a cord? Here, bind him with my scarfe, that wil hold; and yet stand away, Ile doo't my selfe; I cannot trust him with you, least you should let him sometime scape free: besides, you cannot vse him according to the quality of his offence, and because Ile glory in his bondage my chamber shall bee his prison; let him haue neither light, meat, nor drinke, but what I prouide him my selfe.

Hort. Your will's a law, we obey it, madam.

Asp. She knowes me sure ; well, though my ioyes be My comforts this, a speedy death ends all.   [thrall,

                        [*Exit with Hort. and Ass.*

Flo. Oh, you are not gone, then.

Page. Heer's a newe kinde of courting, neuer scene before, I thinke.

Flo. He would anger me.

Pa. Nay, you take a course to anger him first, I thinke.

Flo. Should I haue let him go (as I could no other way detaine him in modesty), and he had set his loue on some other, t'would haue fretted my hart strings a sunder.

Pa. Why did you set him so light, then ?

Flo. Not for any hate, but in pride of my humour.

Page. Why did you commaund him close prisoner to your chamber ?

Flo. That I may feede mine eie with the sight of him, and be sure no other beauty can rob me of his company : I will ha't all, I will not loose an ynch of him. And in this I but imitate our Italian dames, who cause their friends to clap their ielous husbands in prison, that if they haue occasion to vse them within fortie weekes and a day, they may surely know where to find them.   [*Exit.*

Pa. If I had any knauery in mee, as I am all honesty, I could make a notable sceane of mirth betwixt
these two amorists.

Enter Antonio with a net.

Anth. Early sorrow, art got vp so soone?
What, ere the sun ascendeth in the east?
O what an early waker art thou growne!
But cease discourse, and close vnto thy worke;
Vnder this drooping mirtle will I sit,
And worke a while vpon my corded net;
And as I worke, record my sorrowes past,
Asking old Time, how long my woes shall last:
And first,—but stay, alas! what do I see?
Moist gum, like teares, drop from this mournfull tree.
And see, it sticks like birdlyme; twill not part;
Sorrow is euen such birdlyme at my hart.
Alas, poore tree, dost thou want company?
Thou dost, I see't, and I will weepe with thee;
Thy sorrowes make thee dumb, and so shall mine.
It shall be tongueles, and so seeme like thine;
Thus will I rest my head vnto thy barke,
Whilst my sighes tell my sorrowes; harke, tree, harke.

Enter Hippolito and Francisco.

Fr. Fie, fie, how heauy is light loue in me!

Hip. How slow runs swift desire!

Fr. This leaden ayre,
This pondrous feather, merry melancholy.

Hip. This passion, which, but in passion
Hath not his perfect shape.

Fr. And shapelesse loue
Hath in his watch of loue oreslept himselfe.   [der,

Hip. Then, sleepy wakers, let these graue lets wan-
And waite th'ascension of beauties wonder:
But stay, a man striuing twixt life and death.

Fr. Nay, then tis so, my heauenly loue's gone by,
And struck him dead with her loue-darting eye.

Hip. If speech-bereauing loue will let thee speake,
Then, speechles man, speake with the tongue of loue,
And tell me, if thou saw'st not Cynthia
Seeking Endimion in these flowry dales.

Anth. Dales for Endimion and faire Cynthia fit,
But neuer heauenly goddesse blest this groue;
These woods are consecrate to griefe, not loue.

Fr. Out, atheist, thou prophan'st loues deity;
For, false-reporter, I in them haue seene
A loue that makes a negro of loues queene:
One that when as the sunne keeps holliday,
Hir beauty clads him in his best array.   [here;

Anth. Now truly, shepheard, none such soiourn
Please you suruey the cell, go in and see,
I'me hearst, and none but sorrowe lies with me.

                    Enter Lucida.

Fra. Call you this sorrowes caue?

Enter Octauio and whisper with Antonio.

Hip. Rather a cell,

Where pleasure growes, and none but angels dwell.

Fra. To what compare shall I compare thee to?

Vncomparable beauties paragon!

Hip. I will compare her beauty to the sunne,

For her bright lustre giues the morning light.

Fr. Ile say she is like Cynthia when day's done,

Or lady to the mistrisse of the night.

Hip. O speake but to me, and I shall be blest.

Fr. One smile would lay my iarring thoughts at rest.

Enter Hermia.

Her. How now, faire sister? you are hard beset.

Hip. Nymph.

Fr. Goddesse.

Hip. Saynt, once more, y'are both well met.

Fra. O she is faire.

Hip. She fairer.

Fra. Both more faire

Then rocks of pearle, or the chast euening ayre.

Hip. Say, sweet, intend you not to fish to day?

Her. No, shepheards, now fish do not bite but play.

Fr. What time, sweet loue, keepe fishes when they

Luc. Early ith' morning, or els late at night. [bite?

Hip. Come, will you talke with me till time of fishing?

Her. My father, sir, will chide if I be missing.

Oct. The match is made, th'are euen vpon going.

Ant. What should we do?

Oct. Why, as poore parents and dutifull seruants
should doe, run amongst the bushes and catch flies.

Ant. Stay, forward daughters, whether are yee
      going?

Her. Father, I thinke these shepheards come a
      wooing.

Ant. A wooing, daughters? nere imagine so:
What man's so mad to marry griefe and woe?

Fra. Why, where liues sad griefe? heer's all speak-
      ing ioy.

Hip. O, I would liue and die with such annoy.

Ant. But they are poore, and pouerty is despisde.

Hip. No, they are faire, beauty is highly prizde.

Oct. Twill be a match, they are beating the price
      already.   [changd them;

Ant. They once were faire, sorrow from that hath
They once knew wealth, but chance hath much es-
      trangd them.

Fra. Haue they bin faire? what fayrer then they are?
Why tis not possible, this heauenly faire
Hath only in it selfe beauties exceed,
O then rich, fayre, and onely selues exceed.   [please,

Ant. Come, daughters, and come, shepheards, if you
Ile leade you to the lodge of little ease,
Where I will feast you with what cheere I may,
Griefe shall turne mirth, and keepe high holliday.

                          [*Exit cum filiabus.*

The brothers going out, Octauio staies them.

Oct. A word with you ; you meane to marry these wenches ?

Ambo. We doe.

Oct. And are going to contract your selues ?

Ambo. We are.

Hip. And what say you to this ?

Oct. God speede you : I would haue you marry on Saint Lukes day.

Fr. Why ?

Oct. Because I would offer at your wedding.

Fr. Come, th'art all enuy, feed vpon thy hate,
This day our quest of loue shall terminate.

[*Exeunt; manet Octauio.*

Oct. Not if I liue; this maladie of loue
Is grown so strong, it will not be driuen out.
To see the folly of a doating father;
What toyle I had to fashion them to loue,
And how tis doubled to misfashion them.
They shall not wed, yet how shall I preuent it ?
Fearing th'euent, I haue forethought a meanes,
And here it lies ; swaggering becomes not age ;
Now like the fox, ile goe a pilgrimage.
Frollick, my boyes, I come to mar your sport ;
Your country musicke must not play at court.
But first, ile write back to Hortensio
For apprehension of yong Aspero :

They haue not yet dynde, ile bid my selfe their guest :
Religion beg ? a fashion in request.   [*Exit.*

Enter Aspero and his boy.

Asp. Art sure she hates me, boy ?

Boy. More then hir death. I haue bin in hir bosome,
sir ; and this day she intends your execution.

Asp. My execution ! the reason of hir hate ?

Boy. Hir humour ; nothing but a kind of strange
crosse humor in that you reiected hir loue.

Asp. Thats not capitall.

Boy. Not to crosse a great ones humour ? no treason more : great personages humours are puritanes ;
thei'l as liue indure the diuel as soon as a crosse ; and
can away with him better.

Asp. I will submit, aske pardon on my knee.

Boy. Is your proud humour come downe ifaith ;
your high humor that would not stoop an ynch of the
knees ? ile help't vp againe, and't be but to vphold
the icast. I must bring her as low ere I haue done.
O base, I woulde rather lay my necke vnder the axe
of her hate, then my sporte vnder the feete of hir
humor ; but be counselld, ile teach you to preuent both ;
and perchance, make her vpstart humour stoope
gallant, too.

Asp. Ile hold thee my best iewell, and thou dost.

Boy. And pawne me as poore lords do their iewells,

too, will you not? receiue me, you shall counterfet
your selfe dead.

Asp. The life of that ieast?

Boy. It may be, she dissembles all this while; loues
you, and puts on this shew of hate of purpose to
humble you: she may, and I beleeue——

Asp. What?

Boy. That most intelligencers are knaues, and some
women dissemblers; being thought dead (as let me
alone to buz that into the credulous eare of the court)
if she haue any sparkes of loue, theil kindle and flame
bright through the cinders of her hart.

Asp. If not?

Boy. If not, twill be a meanes for your escape: ile
say you requested, at your death, to be buried at your
natiue citty; and what courtier, if a christian, can
deny that?

Asp. I am all thine, my humour's thy patient.

Boy. And if I do not kill it, I am not worthy to be
your physitian.   [*Exeunt.*

Enter Florimell and hir Page.

Pa. I mary, lady; why, now you credit your sex?
a womans honor or humour should be like a ship
vnder saile; split her keele ere she vaile. [*Enter Boy.*

Flo. Ile split my heart, ere my humor strike saile.
Here comes his Page. How now, boy? how doth
your master?

Boy. Well, madam, he.

Flo. Well?

Boy. Very well.

Flo. Where is he?

Boy. Where none of your proude sex will euer come, I thinke: in heauen.

Flo. Is he dead?

Boy. See madam; and seeing blush; and blushing shame, that your vngentle humor should be the death of so good and generous a spirit.

    [*Discouer Aspero lying on a table, seeming dead.*

Flo. My Aspero dead!

Boy. See, madam, what a mutation.

Flo. I see too much; and curse my proude humour that was the cause of it. Aspero, kinde soule; proud sullen Florimell; disdainefull humor, that in one minute hast eternally vndone me: I would not kisse the liuing substance, that being dead, doate on thy picture. O I lou'd thee euer with my soule. O let me kisse this shrowd of beauty. I would not accept thee liuing; that being dead, on my knees adore thee; could kisses recouer thee, I would dwell on thy lips; kneele till my knees grew to the ground, deere, gentle Aspero.

She that procurde thy death, will die with thee;

And craue no heauen, but still to lie with thee.

              [*Aspero starts vp.*

Asp. I take you at your word, lady.

Nay, neuer recant, I haue witnes on't now; is your proude humor come downe? could you not haue said so at first, and sau'd me a labour of dying?

Flo. Liues Aspero?

Asp. Liue quotha? sfoot, what man would bee so mad to lye in his colde graue alone, and may lie in a warme bed with such a beautifull wife as this will be? haue I tane your humour napping yfaith?

Flo. Am I ore reacht?

Asp. In your humour, madam, nothing els; and I am as proude on't.

Flo. Do not flowt me; and you doe, I shall grow into my humour againe.

Asp. In ieast?

Flo. In earnest I shall, and then I know what I know.

Asp. You may; but and you do, I shall die againe.

Flo. In ieast?

Asp. Nay, in earnest, madam, and then——.

Flo. No more; thou hast driuen mee cleane out of conceite with my humor. I loue thee, I confesse it: shalt be my husband, ile liue with thee; thou art my life, and ile die with thee.

What more I meane is coated in my looke,

If thou acceptst it, sweare.

Asp. I kisse the booke.

Flo. Boy, run to the master of my gundelo, and will him attend me after supper at the garden staires ; I meane to take the euening ayre, tell him.

Pa. It shall be done, madam.   [*Exit.*

Flo. Nay, if I say the word, it shall be done Aspero.

Boy. Look to your selfe, my lord ; I lay my life, my lady means to steale you away to night.

Asp. Away ? ile call Hortensio, ile not be accessary to your fellony, madam.

Enter Hortensio, and his man Assistance, with a letter.

Flo. The foole comes without calling.

Ass. You shall know him by these signes.

Hort. Good figure, very good figure ; for as the house is found out by the signe, so must this traytor be sented out by the token ; vp with the first signe, good Assistance.

Ass. A proper man without a beard.

Hor. How, a proper man without a beard ? we shall scarce finde that signe in all Venice : for the propernesse of a man lines altogether in the fashion of his beard ; good Assistance, the next.

Ass. Faire spoken and well conditioned.

Hort. More straunge : you shall haue many proper men fayre spoken, but not one amongst twenty well condicioned : but soft ; this should be the house, by the signe ; I must pick it out of him by wit.

Flo. As good say stcale, my lord; what mary-bone of witte is your iudgement going to pick now?

Hort. I must, like a wise iustice of peace, picke treason out of this fellow.

Flo. Treason?

Hort. I, treason, madam; know you this hand?

Flo. My roiall fathers.

Hor. Then, whilst you and your fathers letters talke togither, let me examine this fellow: are you a proper man without a beard?

Asp. My propernes, sir, contents me: for my beard, indeed that was bitten the last great frost, and so were a number of justices of peace besides.

Hort. Tis rumourd about the court that your name is Aspero.

Asp. I am call'd Aspero.

Hor. Sonne to the duke of Mantua that was?

Asp. The duke of Mantuaes sonne that is.

Hort. Then the duke of Mantua has a traytor to his sonne; lay hands of him, and to close prison with him.

Flo. Can he be closer then in my custody?

Hort. I do not thinke so, madam; but your father has imposde the trust vpon me.

Flo. And dare not you trust mee?

Hor. With my head, if you were my wife; but not with my profit, if you were my mother: will you along, sir?

Asp. With all my heart, sir; see what your humour's come to now: go, my lord? as willingly as a
slaue from the gallies: for as I shall haue a stronger
prison, so I shall bee sure of a kinder and a wiser
iaylor.

Flo. Do you obscrue how he flowts you, my lord?
That I had bin his keeper but one night longer: but
keepe him close, if he escape (though against thy
will) as I am a mayd,—

Hort. A maide against your will.

Flo. —shalt pay as deere for't as thou didst for thy
office.

Hort. If he scape, hang me.

[*Exit and As. with Aspero.*

Flo. I shall wish thee hangd, if he do not: treason!
I may thanke my peeuish humor fort.

Enter Page.

Page. Madam, the gundelo is ready.

Flo. Thou bringst physicke when the patient's dead,
boy: our icast's turnd carnest.

Pa. Is a dead in earnest?

Flo. As good, or rather worse; hee's buried quick.

Pa. O madam, many a good thing has bin buried
quick and suruiu'd againe; I would bee buried quicke
my selfe, and I might choose my graue.

Flo. Hee's buried in close prison, boy; hee's

knowne for the duke of Mantuaes sonne, and by my
fathers letter attached for a traytor.

Pa. Good gentleman, and I be not sorrie for him :
who is his keeper ?

Flo. The testie asse Hortensio.

Pa. Vdsfoot, lets enlarge him.

Flo. Not possible, boy.

Pa. Not possible ? tis : weele cousen his keeper.

Flo. We cannot.

Pa. Cannot! we can : your father made a lord of
him; but be rul'd by me, his daughter shall make a
foole of him. You are not the first woman has made a
foole of a wiser lord then he is.

Flo. Shall he be cousend ?

Pa. As palpably as at the lotterie.   My brains are
in labour of the stratagem alreadie.   [*Exeunt.*

Finis Actus Tertii.

ACTVS QVARTVS.

*Enter Anthonio, Francisco, Hippolito, Hermia, Lucida,
and Octauio disguisd.*

Anth. Sons of Octauio, if your princely thoughts
Can stoope to such meane beauty, from this hand
Receiue your wiues; but should the duke your father—

Fr. Feare not, old man, he was the meanes that
breath'd this spirit into vs.   E

Hip. Wood vs to this course.

But should he prouc apostata, denie

Loue which he first enforcd vs to profes,

So firme are our inseparate affections,

To winne our loues weed loose the names of sonnes.

Oct. Your father thanks you; but, hot-sprighted

Take counsell from experience, ere yee tie　[youthes,

The gordian knot which none but heauen can loose.

Craue his consent : when an imperiall hand

Shakes a weake shed, the building cannot stand.

Fr. Not stand? it shall : not Ioue himselfe can

ruine the ground-worke of our loue.

Oct. Not Ioue!

Hip. Not Ioue,

Should a speak thunder ; then go boldly on,

Our loue admits no separation.

Oct. Then to mine office : in the sighte of heauen

your loue is chast.

Fra. ⎫
　　　⎬ As innocence white soule.
Hip. ⎭

Oct. And yours.

Herm. ⎫
　　　⎬ And ours.
Incid. ⎭

Oct. Then lend me all your hands,

Whilst thus a fathers tongue forbids the bands.

　　　　　　　　[*Discouers himselfe.*

Forgetfull boyes! but most audacious traytor,

That durst in thought consent to wrong thy prince,
Out of my sight; no land that calls me lord
Shall beare a waight so hatefull as thy selfe :
Liue euer banishd.   If (three daies expirde)
Thou or these lustfull strumpets—

    Hip. Father.

       Oct. Boyes,

If you be mine, show't in obedience :
If (three daies past) you liue within my dukedome,
Thee as a slaue ile doome vnto the gallies,
And these thy brats as common prostitutes
Shall drie their lustfull veynes in the Burdello.
Come, boyes, to court; he that first gaue you liues,
Will to your births prouide you equall wiues.

 Fr. They haue our loues.

    Hip. Our oathes.

      Fr. Our hearts and hands.

 Oct. Tut, louers othes, like toyes writ down in sands,
Are soone blowne ore ; contracts are common wiles
T'intangle fooles ; Ioue himselfe sits and smiles
At louers periuries.   Bawd, strumpets hence,
My bosome's chargde, giue way to violence :
Come, doe not mind them.

    [*Exeunt Auth. and his daughters.*

 Fran. How ? not minde them, father ?
When in your court you courted vs to loue,
You red another lecture : women then
Were angells.   E 2

Oct. True, but that was before angells
Had power to make them diuells; they were then
Fiends to themselues, and angells vnto men.
When vpon Po thou find'st a cole-black swan,
Th'ast found a woman constant to a man.

Fr. And not afore?

    Oct. Neuer afore.

      Hip. Your tongue
Vnspeaks your former speech.

       Oct. It doth; new theames
Must haue new change of rhetorique; all streames
Flow not alike one way; when I spake like a louer,
It was to breake you from yonr souldiers humour;
Hauing made you louers, I, like enny, speak
To make you hate loue; art still striues to breake
Bad to make better.

Brothers. You haue your wish.

      Oct. Then onward to the court,
Make vs of loue as schoole-boyes do of sport.

          [*Exeunt.*

   Enter Florimell and her Page.

Flo. Call out the iaylor, boy,—yet doe not; hast
got a beard like Hortensio?

Page. Yes, madam, I haue got his hayre; if I
coulde come as easily by his wit.

Flo. Wouldst rob him of his wit?

Pa. If I shold, he could not hang me for't: tis not worth thirteen pence halfe penny. But what shall I with it?

Flo. Put it on, boy.

Pa. That shall I, madam. O forward age, I am a man already: how do you like me, lady?

Flo. Very ill, and my plot worse.

Pa. Then leaue't of. If you be grounded in the plot, you will but marre the comedy.

Flo. I purposde, thou, in the habit of Hortensio, shouldst vnder pretence of remouing Aspero to a new prison, haue freed him out of the old one.

Pa. Tut, I can tell you a trick worth two of that; madam, your care, take some care in the managing, and let me alone to prepare it. [*Exeunt.*

Enter Aspero and his Boy.

Boy. Vdsfoot, breake prison, my lorde, tis but swimming the riuer.

Asp. Breake prison? twere both dishonour to my name, and treason to my loue; what benefit wer't for me to free my body, and leaue my heart in bondage? ile die, ere ile harbour a disloyall thought.

Pa. It beares no rellish of disloyaltie: being in prison you liue as far from loue as liberty: being abroad, you may by letters, or a thousand meanes, purchase hir company, and compasse your content.

Asp. Shalt be my lawyer, boy, and counsell me.

Boy. Ile looke for my fee, then.

Asp. If thy counsell prospers.

Boy. Thats an exception lawyers neuer respect; but come, my lord, leape; as we haue risen togither, weele fall togither.

Enter Hort., Florimell and Page.

Asp. Blame me not, loue.

Boy. Vdsfoot, your iaylor, my lord.

Asp. Am I preuented?

Boy. Yes faith, there had bin a counsellors fee cast away now.

Hort. You haue heard his vsage, lady, scene his lodging, and if it please you, you both may and shall confer with him.

Flo. Prithee call him.

Boy. My lord, your keeper hath brought a lady or two to see you.

Asp. To see me? why, am I turnd monster? doth he take money to shew me? what doth a take a peece, troe?

Flo. Why, how now, gallant, not gone yet?

Asp. Not, I thanke you, lady, and yet I was neer't.

Hort. How do you, man?

Asp. Musty for want of ayring.

Flo. Weele haue you hangd out i'the fresh ayre one of these mornings.

Asp. Youd be glad to take me in, then,

Flo. Yes, when you had hangd abroad a little : but my lorde Hortensio (for I think I must be your lady when all's done), what sport? I would be merry a purpose to make him mad; the room's priuate and fit for any exercise.

Pa. Vdsfoot to her, can a woman offer fairer for't?

Hort. Why, shall we go to span-counter, madam?

Pa. To span-counter; best ask her, and sheele go to coits.

Flo. No, I loue some stirring exercise; my body's condiciond like the sun, it would neuer be out of motion.

Hor. I hau't, yfaith; when I was student in Padua, we vsde a most ingenious pastime.

Flo. The name, my lord?

Hort. I cannot giue it a name equall to the merit. Tis vulgarly calld Blindmans buffe.

Pa. Blind mans buffe? ha, ha, ha!

Hort. Do you laugh at it?

Flo. At the happines of your wit, my lord, that you shoulde hit vpon that sport, which of all other I delight in.

Hor. Will you heare an apology I made in the commendation of it?

Flo. Weele haue the thing it selfe first ; and as we

like that, weel heare your apologie after: who shall
be hud-winckt first?

Pa. Who, but the author?

Hort. I, I, none shall be blind but I; helpe of with
my gown, boy.

Pa. What shall we haue to blind him?

Flo. My scarfe.   Take my scarfe, my lord.

Pa. There's a simple fauour for you.

Hort. And most fit, for indeed nothing blinds louers
sooner then ladies fauours.   But who shall blind me?

Flo. Mary, that will I, my lord; let me alone to blind
you.

Hort. Good againe; for who should blind men but
beautious women? Come, sweet madam.

Flo. But how if you take me? as I know that will
be your ayme.

Hort. If I take you prisoner, madam, you must
either bee hudwinckt your selfe, or giue your conqueror
a kisse for your ransome.

Flo. An easie ransome : ile not be prisoner long, if
a kisse will enlarge me.

Pa. Lord, what scambling shift has he made for a
kisse, and cannot get it neither ; a little higher, so, so,
so ; are you blind, my lord?

Hort. As a purblind poet : haue amongst you, blind
harpers.

Flo. Me thinks he looks for all the world like God
Cupid.

Pa. Take heed of his dart, madam, he comes vpon you.

Flo. He cannot come to fast. O I am taken prisoner.

Hort. Your ransome's but a kisse.

Flo. Is that your law of armes?

Hort. Yes, madam; but ile take it on your lips.

Flo. My lips, like faithfull treasurers, shall see it discharged.

Hort. And here are my honest receiuers to take it.

[*The Page puts his pantofle to his lips; he kisses it.*

Flo. Am I freed now?

Hort. As if you had seru'd seauen yeare for't: sweete kisse, rare lippe.

Pa. Has she not a sweet breath, my lord?

Hort. As perfume.

Pa. And a soft lip?

Hort. And smooth as veluet; I could scarce discerne it from veluet: ide pawne my office for the fellow on't, madam.

Pa. Here.

Flo. Here, Aspero, on with this beard and gowne: I thinke hee followes me by the sent. His hat, so: a narrow misse yfaith, my lord!

Hort. Gone, madam?

Flo. Euen vpon going. One of you counterfet my my voice. There, I deceiud you, my lord.

Hort. Haue you deceiu'd me, madam?

Flo. Not yet, but I will and you look not the better too't. Busie him till you thinke we are out of the court, and then followe vs: you shall find vs at the south port. Now or neuer, my lord.

Hort. Why then twill neuer be, lady.

Boy. Here.

Hor. Where?

Boy. Here.

Hort. Scapt againe?

Pa. Shee's scapt indeed, my lord; you may cast your cap after her, for I see you can do no other good vpon hir.

Hort. What, haue I catchd you?

Pa. Kisse her and let her goe.

Hort. Kings truce till I breath a little.

Pa. And you had neede so, for I thinke you are almost out of breath; if you be not, you shall be, and thats as good; but breathe and spare not.

*Enter Aspero, like Hortensio, Florimell, and Assistance,
on the vpper stage.*

Asp. Did you euer conuerse with a more straunger dissolute, madam?

Flo. Peremptory iacke, iaylor, as you respect your office, lay speciall watch that none of what degree soeuer haue accesse to him.

Asp. Without me?

Ass. Or your signet.

Asp. Signet mee no signets ; your goldsmiths shop is like your swans neast, has a whole brood of signets, and all of a feather ; and amongst many, one may be like another. Let none enter vpon the stage where Aspero playes the madam, without Hortensio.

Ass. Is he mad, my lord ?

Asp. As the lord that gaue all to his followers, and beg'd more for himselfe.

Flo. If he call for me, tell him I scorne him.

Asp. If he counterfet my voice (as mad fellowes will counterfet great mens hands, and their tongues too) rate him for't, threaten him with the whip.

Flo. But come not at him.

Asp. If he call for meate, promise him faire.

Flo. But giue him none.

Ass. If for light ?

Flo. He may fire the house, let him haue none.

Asp. If he chafe, laugh.

Flo. If he rayle, sing.

Asp. If he speake fayre, flowt him.

Flo. Do anything to vexe him.

Asp. But nothing to content him ; you heare my charge ; as you respect your office, regard it.

Ass. I warne you, my lord, let mee alone, and we knew not how to abuse a prisoner, we were not worthy to be a iaylor.　　　　　　　　　　　　[*Exeunt.*

They renew blind mans buffe on the lower stage.

Pa. Are you in breath, my lord?

Hort. As a bruers horse, and as long winded; looke
to your selfe, madam, I come vpon you.

Boy. I am ready for you, sir; O for a bul-rush to
run a tilt at's nose.

Pa. A fayre misse yfaith.

Hort. Ile mend it next course, you shall see.

Pa. In the corner of the left hand; vdsfoot, ware
shins, my lord.

Hort. Madam.

Boy. Here.

Hort. Where?   [*The boy throwes him downe.*
Helpe me vp, madam.

Boy. O strange! cannot you get vp without helpe?
there's my gloue, but come no neerer, as you loue me.

Hort. I do loue you, madam.

Boy. Oh! blind loue.

Hort. True, madam; your beauty has made me
blind.

Pa. Indeed, loues sonnes like spaniells are all borne
blind.

Hort. But they will see.

Boy. Not till they be nyne daies old, my lord.

Hort. But will you giue mee the fingers that hold
this gloue, madam?

Boy. And the whole body to pleasure you, my lord;
but let me go a little.

Hort. I will not loose you yet, lady.

Boy. But you shall, my lord ; hist, then keepe me
still.   [*He fastens the gloue to a post.*

Pa. Faith, let go, my lord, for she growes sullen,
and you had as goode talke to a post, and as good
answer twould make you.   [*Exeunt.*

Hort. Nay, but deere madam, doe but answer me,
may I presume, vppon my knees I beg it; but to take
a fauour from your sweet lips, shall I ? las, I am not
the first man that loue has blinded. May I presume?
I would be loth to offend your milde patience so
much, as with an unreuerend touch : speake; if I
shall reape the haruest of my honest desires, make me
blest in proposing the time when ; what, not a word ?
are you displeased? or shall I take your silence for a
consent? shall I? speake; or if modesty locke in your
syllables, scale my assurance with a kisse : not neither?
shall I haue neither your word nor your bond? nay,
then I must make bold with modesty ; by this kisse,
madam. O my hard fortune, haue I made suit to
a poast all this while? what block but I would haue
bin so sencelesse? my excuse is, 'twas but to make my
lady sport : and, madam, how ? lady, madam, boy ;
madam, Aspero ! But whist, I haue the conceite, 'twas
excellent in my lady, and I applaud it ; suppose my
lady and hir prisoner had an intent of priuate busines
in the next roome, was it not better in her to blinde me,

then I should as gentlemen vshers (cases so standing),
haue blinded my selfe? againe, I applaud her, and
adore my starres that made me rather a blind then a
seeing dore-keeper: shall I interrupt them? no,
madam; they haue not done yet, sure they haue not.
What haue we here, a base violl? though I cannot
tickle the mynnikyn within, ile (though it be somewhat base) giue them a song without, and the name
of the ditty shall be;

The Gentleman Vshers Voluntarie.

(He sings.)

Peace, peace, peace, make no noyse,

Pleasure and feare lie sleeping.

End, end, end your idle toyes,

Iealous eies will be peeping.

Kisse, kisse and part, though not for hate, for pittie;
Ha done, ha done, ha done, for I ha done my dittie.

And if you haue not done now, too, let me be
as base as my fiddle, if I rowze you not: madam, for
shame, what doe you meane to make of me. How?
sfoote, what haue you made of me already? all gone?
Iaylor?

Enter Assistance aboue.

Ass. How now, who calls?

Hort. Why, saucie knane, tis I.

Ass. You; what you?

Hort. A single V; I came in double, but I thanke them, they are gone out, and left me here a single.——-

Ass. Foole, and so I leaue you.

Hort. Knaue, I am Hortensio; I charge thee let me out.

Ass. Foole, you lye; you are Aspero, and I haue charge to keepe you in.

Hort. From whom?

Ass. From my lord Hortensio.

Hort. Sfoot, knaue, I tell thee I am hee; and thou wilt not beleeue me, trust thine eies, come in and see.

Ass. 'Twill not serue your turne. I like a whole skinne better then a pinkt one: content your selfe to night, and in the morning ile tell you more.

Hort. Where's my lady? send her hither.

Ass. Shee's busie with my lord Hortensio; but if you haue any vse for a woman, ile send you one of the laundresses: fare you well, sir, bee content, you shall want nothing of anything you haue.

Hort. Hortensio gone out! and my ladie busie with Hortensio? I am gulld, palpably gulld: whilst I like a blocke stood courting the post, Aspero is in my apparrell escapde. Villains! traytors! open the doore, the duke's abusd, his daughter's fled: I proclaime yee all traytors that hinder me in the pursuit.

Ass. O for a reasonable audience to applaud this sceane of merryment: ile goe call my lady and my lord Hortensio.   [*Exit.*

Hort. Blindmans buffe ? I haue bufft it fairely, and
mine owne gullery grieues me not half so much as the
dukes displeasure. Iaylor ! not a word ? Iaylor, there's
no way to please a knaue but fayre words, and gold :
honest kinde iaylor, here's gold for thee : doe but
take pittie vpon me, a miserable cony-catchd courtier.
Not? neither fayre nor foule ? thou art a degree worse
then a woman ; what shall I do ? I can compare my
fortune, and my vnfortunate selfe, to nothing so fitlie
as my base here ; wee suffer euery foole to play vpon
vs for their pleasure ; and indeede 'twas the intent of
our Creator that made fiddles and seruitors to nothing
but to be playd vpon, and playd vpon wee shall bee,
till our heart strings crack, and then they either cast
vs aside or hang vs vp, as worthy no other imployment. Well, if I can worke my meanes of escape, so :
if not, I must lie by it.   [*Exit.*

Finis Actus Quarti.

ACTVS QVINTVS.

Enter Octauio, Francisco, Hippolito, Flaminco, &c.

My daughter fled ! and with Hortensio ?
It beares no formall shape of likelyhood ;
Hir eagle spirit soard to proud a pitch,
To seize so base a prey ; let priuy searche

Look through the eitties bosome till they find her :
For gone she is not.

   Fr. Has not Anthonies sonne
Sent them by some base practise to their death ?

  Oct. His breasts too full of honor. Trusty Iulio !

Enter Iulio.

What waighty businesse drawes thee from thy eharge ?

  Iul. Came not the cause afore me ? the proud
Basely reuolt, deposde me from the seate [Mantuans
And chayre of regentship, sending in quest
Of proude Anthonio their late-banisht duke ;
Him if they find or Aspero his sonne,

[*Enter Assist.*

Theile reinstall him in the regiment.

  Oct. Him let them seeke in the vast shades of
death. As for his sonne—

  Ass. Hee's sure ynough, my lord ; he was a mad
knaue when he came in, but I thinke I haue made a
tame foole of him by this time : for a has neither had
bread nor water these foure and forty houres.

  Oct. More villain thou.

  Ass. My lord, Hortensio was the villain ; ho left
such command with mee ; hee's the wheele that
turnes about, and I, a country lack, must strike when
I am commanded.

  Oct. Although my foe, hee's honorably tempred,

F

Yet armd against my life : goe call him forth,
Guard in my safety with a ring of steele,
And marke how proudly heele demeane reuenge.

*Enter Assistance, and Hortensio bareheaded with
his crowd.*

Ass. Goblius, spirits, furies, faeryes! the prison is
haunted!

Oct. With a knaue, is't not?

Ass. Yes, and an olde foole, my lorde, in the likenesse of Hortensio.

Oct. Villain, where's Aspero?

Ass. I know not, my lord : I let him in and my
lady to laugh at him; and it seemes, he consented to
treason, and let him out in his apparrell.

Hor. They consented togither to cousen me : for
taking delight (as my betters may doe) in a foolish
pastime called blindmans buffe, they stole away my
gowne, escapt the prison, and left mee in fooles para-
dice, where what song I haue playd my violl can
witnesse. They made me a little better then a bawd,
my lord.

Fr. In act.

Hort. Not meerly in act : *sed cogitatione, et id satis
est vt inquit Suetonius.*

Oct. Is hee escapt, and Florimell with him? Hortensio, thy head shall answer it.

Hort. I pray let my tongue be my heads atturney,
and pleade my excuse.

Oct. Vrge no excuse. Away with him to prison.

Ass. It shall be done, my lord.

Oct. Nay, you, sir, too, shall taste of the same
sauce ; away with both.

Flamineo. Come, my sonnes,
Lets leauy present armes gaynst Mantua.
Being scarce come home, we must abroad againe ;
The common good's a carefull princes payne.

[*Exeunt.*

Enter Anthonio, Lucida, Hermia, and Lords.

Anth. You that in all my banisht pilgrimage
Would neuer alienate your naturall loues,
But in desire to see me reinstalld
Haue thrust out proude Octauioes substitute,
And seated me in antient dignity,
I am yours, and ready at your best dispose.

Lord. Your owne, my liege, we like inferiour lights
Take life from your reflection, for like stars
Vnto the sunne, are counsellours to kings :
He feeds their orbes with fier, and their shine
Contend to make his glory more diuine.
And such are we to great Anthonio.

Anth. The veynes and arteries of Anthonio
Through which the bloud of greatnesse flows in vs.

Our life, and cause efficient of our state,
And these our prety partners in exile.

    Lord. We ha yet performd but the least part of
        duetie,
Your reinstalment : it rests, that with our bloud
We keepe out innouasiue violence.

    Ant. You new-create me, and breath second life
Into my dying bosome ; knew my sonne
Of this vnlookt-for fortune ; but ill fate
Hast playd the traytor, and giuen vp his life
To coward treason.   (*A shout within.*)

   Enter Aspero and Florimell with their Pages.

    Asp. Vdsfoot, what offence haue I committed against
the state, that these yron-handed plebeians so applaud
me for ?

    Flo. Tis a signe they loue you.

    Asp. I had rather they should hate me ; it makes
mee suspect my bosome ; for they loue none but the
masters of factions, treasons, and innouasions.

    Flo. Then you doe not loue the commons.

    Asp. Yes, as wise men doe their flattering wiues,
only for show : the popular voyce is like a crie of
bauling hounds ; and they get the foote of a fantas-
ticke and popular-affecting statesman, they neuer
leaue him, till they haue chac'd him into disgrace,
and then, like hounds, are at a losse, and with their

losse—See, I haue found my father. Safety attend
you.

Anth. Welcome, thou hope of Mantua and of vs.
We now are honors new-beginners, boy,
And may we better thriue then heretofore.

Asp. Neuer doubt it, father ; I haue attractiue stuffe
that will draw customers.

Anth. What lady's that ?

Flo. One that has playd the part of a constable,—
brought you home a runaway.

Asp. A friend of mine, father, but daughter to your
arch-enemy.

Anth. Octauioes daughter ?

Asp. Yes faith ; you are out with the father, and ile
see if I can fall in with the daughter.

Flo. And am I not a good child to leaue my fathers
loue at sixe and seauen, and hazard my honor vpon
your sonnes naked promise, and your hopefull ac-
ceptance.

Asp. She has followed me through much danger.

Anth. The better welcome ; I loue her for't.

Asp. Like her and you please, id'e haue no body
loue her but my selfe.

Anth. And, lady, though your father be our foe,
The vertuous loue betwixt our sonne and you,
May nerethelesse retaine his simpathie.

Flo Shall nerethelesse retaine his simpathy ;
Anthonio, know I am loues resolute,

Confirmd and grounded in affection:
I lou'd your sonne, not for he was a prince,
But one no better then his present fortunes,
Ile loue him still, since first I lou'd him so,
Let father, friends, and all the world say no.

Asp. There's mettle, father; how can wee choose
but get cocking children, when father and mother too
are both of the game.

Enter Messenger.

Mess. To armes, my lord; Octauio comes in armes,
To giue a proud assault vnto the citty.

Asp. Proud his assault, as proud be our resist,
Vye shot for shot, and stake downe life for life,
Our brest's as bold as theirs, our bloud as deepe,
All that wee'l loose, or this our gettings keepe.

Her. Come, brother, talke not of deuouring war
Say, messenger, comes not Octauioes sonnes ?

Mess. They do, as proudly as the morning sunne
Beating the azurd pauement of the heauen.

Her. Then feare not, father, my sister and my selfe
Will be your champions, and defend the citty.

Flo. Why, ladies, haue you such large interest in
our brothers ?

Fr. Princesse, we haue.   Within there : reach our
          shields ;
When beauty fights, the God of battaile yeelds.

                              [*Exeunt.*

Enter Francisco, Hippolito, Flamineo, Iulio.
Enter Anthonio, Aspero, Florimell, two Pages, Lords and
Messenger aboue.

Flo. They offer parlee, let me answer them.
Brothers, how now? who made you souldiers?
Faith een my father, as he made you louers?
What, hath he chang'd your shepheards hooks to
Of Amoradoes made you armed knights? [swords?
O seld-scene metamorphosis! I haue knowne
Souldiers turne louers, but for amorous louers
To re-assume their valour, tis a change
Like winter-thunder, and a thing as strange.

Fr. Our sister prisoner?

Hip. Tell me, Florimell,
Dost thou liue there enforc'd, or of free-will?

Flo. Freewill, brothers, mine owne freewill; all free
in Mantua; here's freewill yfaith, speake, am I not a
free-woman?

Pa. As if you had seru'd for't; any man may set vp
under hir copy without a protection.

Fr. I, wag, are you there too?

Pa. Yes, faith, my lord; my lady has had my atten-
daunce to a hayre.

Flo. You lie, boy.

Pa. If not mine, some bodies els: there's one has
done——.

Asp. What haue I done, sirra?

Pa. Nay nothing, but what my lady was very well content with.

Fr. Why, sister, shame you not to set your loue
On one that is our fathers enemie.

Flo. Shame? not a whit. But come, your wenches,
　　　　brothers;
I make no question, I haue won my wager,—
Are they as faire as I?

Hip. Leaue that to triall.
Aspero, make surrender of our sister.

Asp. And haue her in quiet possession? what do you thinke me?

Fr. We thinke thee a proud villain, and our foe.

Flo. By heauen, th'are villains all that thinke him so.

Hip. Why, doe you loue him?

　　　　　　　Flo. I should curse my selfe
If I should hate him.

　　　　　　　Fr. Bring the ladders forth;
Brauely assault to separate their liues.

　　[*As they are scaling the walls, the ladies come forth.*

Her. Stand, proud Francisco.

Pa. Stand! O excellent word in a woman.

Inc. Hold, Hippolito.

Pa. Hold! vp with that word, and tis as good as the other.

Fr. What nymphe or goddesse in my Hermiaes
Stands to debar my entrance to the towne?　[*shape,*

Pa. Madam, I wonder they enter not.

Flo. Why, boy, it seemes they dare not.

Pa. O cowards, and haue two such fayre breaches

Fr. Immortall Pallas, that art more diuine, [already.

In my loues beautie, than thou cloth'st thee in ;

Withdrawe thy selfe, and giue our fury limits.

Her. I will ; but first, Francisco, take my shielde.

Luc. And mine, as challenge to a single combat.

Her. Read the conditions, and returne your answers.

Flo. Well done, yfaith, wenches. O that the olde
gray-beard, my father, were here ! ide haue a bout
with him, as I am honourable.

Fr. Whats here ?

A shepheard wooing of a countrymaide,

As she sits angling by a riuers side ;

By them an aged man making a net ?

The motto : *Sic !* this emblems morrall is,

The former loue I had with Lucida,

And this hope tells me that's faire Lucida.

Hip. Brother, my shield the like presents to me,

But holds far more familiar reference ;

Here doth the amorous shepheard kisse the nymph ;

Which she with a chast blush consents vnto :

And see, a gloomy man, clad like a pilgrim,

Comes in, and seperates their sweete delights :

The motto, *Sic !* I, so my father came,

And banisht me from beautious Hermia ;

And this, hope tells me, is faire Hermia.

Fr. The more I looke, the more me thinkes tis she.

Hip. The more I think, the more I find tis she.

Fr. What should I thinke, to proue it is not she?

Flo. Looke, thinke, find, proue, do what you can,

These are the wenches that you courted than :

Then, hony bees, lay by your smarting stings,

And buz sweet loue into your ladies eares ;

Tell them of kisses, and such prety things ;

These drumming dub adubs loues pleasure feares.

Fr. O heauen, oh fortune, and most happie stars;

Do I find loue, where I expected wars ?

Hip. I that but now was all for war and death,

Am made all loue ; wars humour's out of breath.

Enter Octauio, Iulio, and others.

Oct. How, my sonnes loue the daughters of my
foe ? it cannot be.

Iul. Then question them your selfe.

Oct. Why, how now, sonnes ? is this your worth in

Fr. Why, are we not in armes, father ?   [armes ?

Hip. Yes, and in such armes as no coward but
woulde venture life to march in.

Oct. Then, boies, you loue the daughters of Anthonio?

Fr. We lik'd them first.

Hip. We keepe that liking still.

Oct. And you will loue them ?

Flo. Father, infaith they will.

Oct. I, runaway, are you there? whome has your ladyship got to your husband?

Flo. One that I stumbled on at blindman buffe; a proper man, a man euery ynch of him: and you would say so and you knewe but asmuch as I——meane to know ere I haue done with him.

Oct. Is he not sonne vnto Anthonio?

Asp. Great duke, I am, and prostrate on my knee,
I beg a peace, which if your spleene deny,
I proudlie stand where erst I mildly kneel'd,
And cast downe bold defiance from theis walls.

Oct. No more: your loues make my proud hart
    asham'd;
Your consort's sweet, and ile not be a meane
To make it iar: what my sonnes like shall stand,
By my consent, allowed and perfected;
All hate is banisht, and reuenge lies dead.

Asp. Then, stead of speares, let Hymens torches
    flame
With hallowed incence; and the God of spright,
Swell vp your vaines with amorous delight:
And so shut vp our single comedy,
With Plautus phrase: *Si placet, plaudite.*

                  [*Exeunt omnes.*

FINIS.

NOTES.

Page 2, line 17. *Aurum Potabile*. This was one of the medicines of the ancient alchemists. It is thus alluded to in Ashmole's *Theatrum Chemicum Britannicum*, 1652, p. 422,—

> And then the golden oyle called *aurum potabile*,
> A medicine most mervelous to preserve man's health.

Page 14, line 26. *But I must play Dun*. This refers to the old rural pastime of drawing Dun out of the mire. The mode of playing it is thus described by Gifford,—A log of wood is brought into the midst of the room. This is Dun, the cart-horse, and a cry is raised that he is stuck in the mire. Two of the company advance, either with or without ropes, to draw him out. After repeated attempts, they find themselves unable to do it, and call for more assistance. The game continues till all the company take part in it, when of course Dun is extracted; and the merriment arises from the awkward and affected efforts of the rustics to lift the log, and sundry arch contrivances to let the ends of it fall on one another's toes.

Page 17, line 24. *Upright shoes*. Meaning straight shoes, those that will fit either foot. It is curious that, in Dr. Johnson's time, the fashion of wearing shoes fitted for the right and left feet had so completely gone out of fashion that Shakespeare's allusion to the practice created a difficulty with the commentators, whose notes on the subject, here subjoined, are somewhat amusing. The passage illustrated is an allusion in *King John* to slippers "hastily thrust upon contrary feet."

I know not how the commentators understand this important passage, which, in Dr. Warburton's edition, is marked as eminently beautiful, and, on the whole, not without justice. But Shakspeare seems to have confounded the man's shoes with his gloves. He that is frighted or hurried may put his hand into the wrong glove, but either shoe will equally admit either foot. The author seems to be disturbed by the disorder which he describes. JOHNSON.

Dr. Johnson forgets that ancient *slippers* might possibly be very different from modern ones. Scott, in his *Discoverie of Witchcraft*, tells us : "He that receiveth a mischance will consider, whether he put not on his shirt wrong side outwards, or his *left shoe* on his *right foot*." One of the jests of Scogan, by Andrew Borde, is how he defrauded two shoemakers, one of a *right foot* boot, and the other of a *left foot one*. And Davies, in one of his Epigrams, compares a man to a " soft-knit *hose, that serves out each leg*." FARMER.

In *The Fleire*, 1615, is the following passage : " — This fellow is like your *upright shoe*, he will serve either foot." From this we may infer, that some shoes could only be worn on the foot for which they were made. And Barrett, in his *Alvearie*, 1580, as an instance of the word *wrong*, says : " — to put on his *shooes wrong*." Again, in *A merye Jest of a man that was called Howleglas*, bl. l., no date : " Howleglas had cut all the lether for the *lefte foote*. Then when his master sawe all his lether cut for the *right foote*, then asked he Howleglas if there belonged not to the *lefte foote* a *right foote*. Then sayd Howleglas to his maister, If that he had tolde that to me before, I would have cut them ; but an it please you I shall cut as mani *right shoone* unto them." Again, in Frobisher's *Second Voyage for the Discoverie of Cataia*, 4to., bl. l.,

1578: "They also beheld (to their great maruaille) a dublet of canuas made after the Englishe fashion, a shirt, a girdle, three shoes for *contrarie feet*," &c. p. 21. See also the *Gentleman's Magazine*, for April, 1797, p. 280, and the plate annexed, figure 3. STEEVENS.

Page 50, line 2. *Apostata.* It was often the practice to write these kind of words in their original form. So, in Massinger's *Unnatural Combat*,—" to punish this apostata with death."

Page 51, line 20. *Jove himself sits.* Originally from Ovid. Greene uses the idea in his *Metamorphosis*,—" What! Eriphila, Jove laughs at the perjurie of lovers."

> And I will take thy word : yet, if thou swear'st,
> Thou may'st prove false; at lovers' perjuries,
> They say, Jove laughs.—*Romeo and Juliet*, ii, 2.